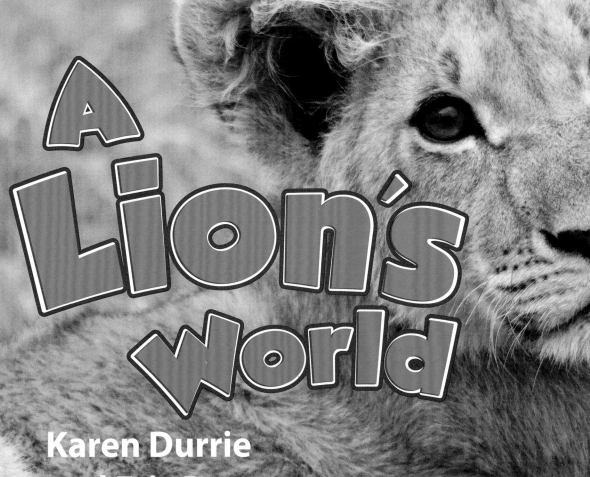

A Lion's World

**Karen Durrie
and Eric Doty**

EYEDISCOVER

EYEDISCOVER

Go to www.eyediscover.com and enter this book's unique code.

BOOK CODE

K 6 6 4 6 7 4

EYEDISCOVER brings you optic readalongs that support active learning.

Published by AV² by Weigl
350 5th Avenue, 59th Floor New York, NY 10118
Website: www.eyediscover.com

Library of Congress Control Number: 2015951240

ISBN 978-1-4896-4103-8 (hardcover)

Printed in the United States of America
in Brainerd, Minnesota
1 2 3 4 5 6 7 8 9 0 20 19 18 17 16

012016
011816

Project Coordinators: Jared Siemens and Katie Gillespie
Designer: Mandy Christiansen

Weigl acknowledges Getty Images and iStock as the primary image suppliers for this title.

EYEDISCOVER provides enriched content, optimized for tablet use, that supplements and complements this book. EYEDISCOVER books strive to create inspired learning and engage young minds in a total learning experience.

Watch
Video content brings each page to life.

Browse
Thumbnails make navigation simple.

Read
Follow along with text on the screen.

Listen
Hear each page read aloud.

Your EYEDISCOVER Optic Readalongs come alive with...

Audio
Listen to the entire book read aloud.

Video
High resolution videos turn each spread into an optic readalong.

OPTIMIZED FOR

- ☑ TABLETS
- ☑ WHITEBOARDS
- ☑ COMPUTERS
- ☑ AND MUCH MORE!

A Lion's World

In this book, you will learn about

- how I look
- where I live
- what I do

and much more!

5

My big, strong legs help me run as fast as a race horse.

My long, thick mane tells other lions I am very powerful.

13

My family is called a pride. We greet each other by rubbing heads.

15

21

LIONS BY THE NUMBERS

There are only about **500** **Asian lions** left in nature.

Fewer than **20,000** lions may live in Africa today.

A lion can run up to **50 miles** per hour.

(80 kilometers per hour)

A lion may **sleep** for **20 hours** each day.

Male lions eat **15 pounds of meat each day.** (7 kilograms)

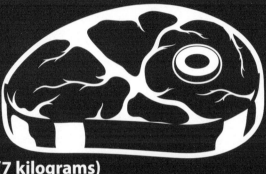

There are about **15 LIONS** in a pride.

23

KEY WORDS

Research has shown that as much as 65 percent of all written material published in English is made up of 300 words. These 300 words cannot be taught using pictures or learned by sounding them out. They must be recognized by sight. This book contains 36 common sight words to help young readers improve their reading fluency and comprehension. This book also teaches young readers several important content words, such as proper nouns. These words are paired with pictures to aid in learning and improve understanding.

Page	Sight Words First Appearance
4	a, am, I
7	in, of, one, the, world
8	away, be, can, from, heard, miles, my
11	as, big, help, me, run
12	long, other, tells, very
15	by, each, family, heads, is, we
16	food, for, groups
19	keep, our, young

Page	Content Words First Appearance
4	lion
7	cats
8	roar
11	horse, legs
12	mane
15	pride
16	females
19	cubs
20	beasts, king

I am a lion.

Watch
Video content brings each page to life.

Browse
Thumbnails make navigation simple.

Read
Follow along with text on the screen.

Listen
Hear each page read aloud.

EYEDISCOVER

Go to www.eyediscover.com and enter this book's unique code.

BOOK CODE

K 6 6 4 6 7 4